BRIGHT SMILE

A SWEET SAPPHIC INTERRACIAL ROMANCE

ROXIE CLARKE

1

DAPHNE SAT atop the six-foot ladder, twisting strands of red, pink, and white lights together. She'd hung heart-shaped wooden frames along the front window of the Secondhand Rose Vintage Thrift Shop and was going to add the lights to the hearts... somehow. She hadn't quite figured that out yet, but she could see the display in her mind and that was as good a place to start as any.

"I don't know how you can sit up there so calmly and work," her boss Maryann said, hand on her hip, looking up at Daphne.

Daphne shrugged. "I spent a lot of time in trees as a kid." Well, that wasn't entirely true. She'd climbed the big oak out behind her duplex just last week.

"The window is looking cool. I'm not a data gal, but I feel like business has picked up since you improved the shop's window dressing game." Maryann smiled at Daphne's handiwork.

"Thank you," Daphne said. "Does this praise come with a raise?"

Maryann tipped her head to the side, thinking. "You and Belle are both due in March for your yearly evals, aren't you?"

"Yeah," Daphne replied, stooping over and winding the lights around the top of the biggest heart.

"I'll see what my accountant says about adding another dollar an hour to your pay."

Daphne grinned. Maryann already paid well but knew the key to keeping her employees happy was actually listening to them and letting them innovate.

Daphne wasn't much of a "data gal" either, but every single customer who came into the Secondhand Rose commented on her windows. Daphne drew them in, and Belle usually made the sales. Maryann took care of all the special orders and finding the perfect wedding gowns. They were a pretty amazing team.

Tabitha, the event planner for the Braverton Botanical Garden, came to a halt in front of the shop window, her head bent over at Daphne's feet level.

Daphne waved a sneakered foot at her, but Tabitha was engaged in some serious texting and not paying attention. Which was okay with Daphne because it let her admire the beautiful woman before her. Brown skin, soft, curly black hair, and a bright smile that lit up her whole face. *Usually*. At the moment, Tabitha's lips were pressed together in a straight line.

Daphne had been crushing on Tabitha for a few months now but couldn't determine if she dated women or not. As far as she knew, Tabitha was single. During the short conversations they'd had in the store she hadn't once casually mentioned having a partner.

"I get what you see in her," Maryann said, dragging Daphne back to the present. "She's got fantastic style. I wish she'd sell some of her vintage dresses to us. I could get good money for all of her Sixties mini-shifts."

"Yeah, but then I wouldn't get to appreciate them on her. That yellow one with the white diamond pattern and the Peter Pan collar is my fave." Daphne finished twisting the lights around the big heart, leaving the rest of the strands dangling. "Will you hold the ladder, please?"

Maryann took hold of it and Daphne climbed down.

Belle walked out from behind the counter where she'd been organizing bags. "Oh, yay! Tabitha's coming to see us."

"Dibs," Daphne said. She cleared her throat. "Did I just say that?"

Belle and Maryann laughed.

"You totally just said that." Belle backed up behind the counter. "I'll be over here organizing, uh, the pens or something with great concentration."

Maryann snorted. "And I'll be in my office staring blankly at my computer screen and thinking about what Luis is bringing me for lunch. I hope it's last night's left over camarones al mojo de ajo."

"Yumtown, population you," Daphne said, smoothing her hands down the front of her black boucle sweater set.

&a.

TABITHA SHOVED her phone into her red pleather tote, banning it to the abyss. She knew she shouldn't shoot the messaging device, but lately all the stupid thing did was deliver bad news.

She brought her head up and found she was looking through a gigantic lighted heart directly at Daphne, who was behind the counter smiling back at her.

Tabitha laughed and went into the shop. "Hey," she said.

"Hey," Daphne said. "Here to pick up this wedding dress?" She nodded toward the dress hanging on the rack next to the counter.

"Yep. The wedding isn't until this evening, but the bridal party is arriving three hours early. So, here I am to pick up that dress." Tabitha took a step closer to the counter, pulling her tote higher up onto her shoulder. She let her gaze fall to Daphne's chin. Tabitha had a hard time looking Daphne in the eyes. She was so pretty. "I love your sweater. You look great in that color."

"Black?" Daphne asked.

"Yep," Tabitha said, tightening her grip on the straps of her tote. She wished she could pause this embarrassing interaction, rewind to a minute ago, and start over. She had definitely spoken to other people before, right? Like, on a daily basis?

Daphne grinned and leaned forward, resting her elbow on the counter, her cute chin in her cute hand. "Thanks. That's so sweet of you. Black is my favorite color."

"Black isn't a color, ladies," Belle said, with her back to them, deep into organizing something. It sort of looked like she was putting the same three pens into a green hobnail milk glass vase and taking them out again. Tabitha couldn't quite see around Daphne, who'd scooted over a couple inches into her field of view.

Belle suddenly yelped, picked up the vase and three pens. "I have to merchandise these over by the girdles."

"So," Daphne said.

"So." Tabitha forced herself to meet Daphne's gaze. The twinkle lights in the window reflected in her dark brown eyes. "Hey, can I ask–"

"I'd love to." Daphne straightened and

pulled her phone from the back pocket of her denim skirt. "What are you thinking? Coffee? Dinner?"

"Um," Tabitha said, her mind struggling to shift gears from work mode where she'd been at the beginning of the question to love life mode where she was right now. She couldn't be here now! Work mode had to take precedence. Today she needed to keep her job more than she needed a girlfriend. Girlfriend? Date. Ack. Work mode! "Hey, um, we should totally get coffee sometime, but I actually was wondering if you could help me set up for tonight's wedding this afternoon?"

Daphne stared at her phone in her hand, her thumb hovering over the screen mid-scroll. "Oh. I thought you were asking me out. Oops!" She giggled, sighed, and then put her phone back into her pocket. "You need me to help you set up for a wedding?"

Tabitha nodded. "The lighting specifically. The guy that was supposed to do it fell off a ladder and broke his shoulder and his leg." She set her tote on the counter and pulled out a blue folder. "I have his plans. It shouldn't be too difficult. You would be doing me a huge favor. And I'd pay you, of course."

Daphne took the folder and perused the plans. "You need this done by tonight?"

"Yep," Tabitha said. "If you could come help, like, right now–"

"Maryann," Daphne called toward her boss' office.

Maryann poked her head out. "What's up?"

Daphne waved her to the counter. "Tabitha needs help with lighting a wedding this afternoon. Is it okay if I take off early?"

"Are you trying to poach my employee?" Maryann asked, her hands on her hips and a wry smile on her lips.

"Just for today," Tabitha said. "My lighting guy is broken and my job is on the line."

"What?" Maryann asked, her shoulders slumping. "You do such good work."

Tabitha rolled her eyes and then took the folder from Daphne. "Well, a certain board member at the garden has a wife that would like my job and I recently lost a big client because they thought my approach to event planning was too 'youthful,' so I get the feeling if I screw up again, it's back to the info desk for me." And back to her basement bedroom at her parents' house.

"That's the pits, kid," Maryann said. "Daph, we can spare you for one afternoon. Go."

Daphne came around the counter and hugged Maryann's shoulders. "Thank you. You're the best. A literal champion."

Maryann laughed and shook her fist in the air like a boxer.

"Let me get my coat." Daphne hurried to the rear of the shop.

"Yes, thank you so much," Tabitha said. "Let me know if I can return the favor."

Maryann took the wedding dress from the rack and handed it to her. "I'd love a pair of tickets to the Valentine's Day event at the garden. It seems like a romantic place to pop a question, doesn't it?"

Tabitha clapped her hands. "You got it." *Finally.* Everyone in Braverton had been speculating if Maryann and Luis were going to tie the knot again. Hopefully this attempt would be more successful. "I'll make sure Luis gets the tickets this evening."

"Fantastic."

Daphne returned wearing a black swing coat, buttoned up crooked, and a stiff proper ladies' pocketbook hung from her arm. "Ready Freddy?"

Tabitha bit the inside of her bottom lip to keep her smile in check. Daphne was SO CUTE. She was bound to freak her out with the full-on goofy grin her mouth wanted to make. "Ready."

"Good luck," Maryann said, shooing them out the front door.

Daphne strutted. "We don't need luck. We've got skills."

Tabitha chuckled behind her.

Daphne turned to her, joining in, and then shrugged. "Intermediate skills."

2

___

DAPHNE HAD DITCHED Broken Shoulder Guy's plans immediately. In her opinion, his designs lacked flair and imagination and smacked of standard issue cis het white dude thinking he's innovative but really, really not, mediocrity.

She stood at the top of the aisle and scrutinized her work above the altar.

"Wowza," Tabitha said, walking up next to her, their shoulders brushing against one another for a moment. "I think Brian was just gonna, like, hang some lights underneath the floral arch. You made it look like fairies are frolicking with fireflies in a field of poppies."

Daphne's mouth dropped open. "That's what I was going for. Well, pixies instead of fairies, but I don't even know the difference between them, so, spot on as far as I'm concerned."

Tabitha let loose a deep, throaty laugh that made Daphne's ears tickle. "I don't know the difference either," she said, striding down the aisle. "One is more mischievous than the other?"

Daphne followed her, mischievous thoughts of what would happen if she reached out and took Tabitha's hand popping into her head. *Better not.* She'd already royally embarrassed herself once today.

"Oh, my goodness gracious," said a high-pitched female voice from the entrance into the garden's atrium.

Tabitha turned; her face lit up with that bright smile Daphne adored. "What do you think?" she asked.

The bridal party rushed past Daphne toward the floral arch, oohing and ahhing over her work.

"It's MA. GI. CAL," the bride said, her outstretched open palms accenting each syllable of the word. "A hundred times better than I thought it was going to be."

"Right?" Tabitha said, gesturing to Daphne. "Brian had a fall, so I asked my friend Daphne to help."

Her friend? Friend was more intimate than acquaintance.

The bride approached Daphne with such enthusiasm that she froze.

"Brian who? Brian's fired," the bride said, grasping Daphne's shoulders. "You are amazing." She blinked away the tears pooling in her heavily made-up eyes. "I'm going to marry the love of my life under a literal work of art. What a gift."

Daphne patted the bride's hand and slowly backed away. Was it obvious her face was on fire? "You're sweet. I have intermediate skills."

"Whatever," one of the bridesmaids said, her frosted blond hair piled high on her head. "You two make a great team."

The bridal party moved *en masse* out to the lobby to get changed.

Tabitha did a happy dance and then pretended to wipe sweat from her brow.

Daphne joined her next to the arch. "I

think it's safe to say, Tabitha, one, board member's wife, zero."

"Fingers crossed." Tabitha looked at her for a moment, her gaze moving from Daphne's chin to meet her eyes. "Two questions this time."

Daphne locked her mouth and threw the invisible key over her shoulder.

"I've got another wedding next week, same time, same place. I'm sure Brian will have to sit that one out too. Want to work with me again?"

Daphne made to search the floor behind her for the key, found it, and unlocked her mouth. "I would love to. This has been a lot of fun."

Tabitha took a step toward her.

"What's the second question?" Daphne took a step toward Tabitha until they were only inches apart.

"Want to be my date to the reception tonight?"

"So I can help clean up?" Daphne asked. "You said date, but I don't want us to get our signals crossed."

"Nah," Tabitha said. "The tear down is

faster than the set up. I want you to be my date... to be my date."

Daphne grinned wide. "Okay, then. I'll be back at seven o'clock. What's the dress code?"

"The bride requested I call it Bohemian Formal on the invitations." Tabitha shrugged. "Whatever that means to you, I'm sure it will be perfect."

"Perfect."

❧

DAPHNE THREW the rear door of the Secondhand Rose open, shucking her coat onto the floor by Maryann's office as she headed for the formal wear. "Belle! Maryann! I need you!"

The women were next to her in a flash, flanking her. "Are you all right?" Maryann asked.

"Tabitha invited me to the wedding reception tonight and the dress code is Bohemian Formal, and I acted like I know what that means, but I don't know what that means. At. All."

Belle elbowed her away from the rack.

"Step aside. I got you." She began pulling dresses in shades of mauve and gold and handing them to Maryann.

Daphne exhaled. She trusted Belle's aesthetic and suspected she came from money, which was why she was so good at selling and why she understood what rich ladies meant when they mixed two opposite vibes together, deeming it a thing.

Belle put a finger to her lips and studied Daphne for a moment. "Do you think you have enough hair to conceal a battery pack?"

"Of course," Daphne said. "Now you're speaking my language."

TABITHA FINISHED ATTACHING the gold lame cape to the shoulders of her cream, peach, and butter yellow rose printed jumpsuit, gave herself a final once over in the bathroom mirror, and then headed out to the atrium to check on everything before she went to meet the bridal party.

The ceremony was scheduled to begin promptly at six o'clock and she'd given Tom and his security team instructions to hold any latecomers in the garden lobby until the bride had made her entrance.

"Ten minutes to go time," Tabitha said into her headset. It was a truly helpful device, but it messed with her hairdo. She hoped she'd have a quick moment to fluff her fro before Daphne arrived.

"Copy that," Tom said. "By the way, Tab, we're all pulling for you and think you do a superb job. I can have Layla ask Bradley to talk to Tyler about buying his way onto the board, maybe nudging Cromwell into early retirement if you want."

Tabitha's eyes flitted around the atrium, checking, checking, checking. "That totally didn't sound like you were going to ask your sister's husband to have his billionaire buddy put a hit out on a board member," she whispered.

Tom laughed. "You know what I meant. What's the use in having a rich guy family adjacent if you can't help out your friends with his money, power, and flair for the dramatic?"

Tyler was Tom's brother-in-law, Bradley's, best friend and he'd once flown a local groom to a wedding at the garden in a helicopter, dressed as Santa Claus.

"I appreciate the thought, sort of, and the support, genuinely, but I think I've got a secret weapon all my own. Did you see the lighting on the altar?" The pre-ceremony music was at the right volume, the guests seemed to be comfortable and were chatting quietly amongst themselves.

"Yeah, Brian really outdid himself. Why has he been holding back?"

"He hasn't. The work was done by Daphne – that cute Korean woman who works at Secondhand Rose." Tabitha took in the altar again. The twinkling lights intertwined with real moss and an array of flowers in various stages of bloom was spectacular.

"Ah, cute, huh?" Tom asked. "I saw on the guest list she was your plus one. I'm pulling for you there, too, then."

Tabitha grinned. Tom had certainly loosened up since high school. She guessed that's what happened when G.I. Joe got tangled up with Ms. Namaste. "You're not going to warn me against blurring the lines between my work life and my love life?"

"That would be hypocritical of me, wouldn't it? Besides, lots of people meet their partners at work."

"Speaking of work. Eight minutes to go time. I'm on my way to corral the bridal party. Hustle any stragglers into the atrium now."

She could practically hear Tom's posture snap to attention. "Lobby is all clear and all ceremony guests are checked in. You're good to go."

3

———————

DAPHNE MILLED about the lobby with the few other guests who were only attending the reception, casually glancing at the different displays and photos without really taking them in.

A man sidled up to her. "Excuse me," he began.

"I'm here on a date," she said without really taking him in either.

He chuckled. "I know. Tab asked me to have you meet her outside by the taco truck in five minutes."

Daphne was grateful she'd taken Belle's advice and gone easy on the blush. "Oh, sorry, I..." She took a good look at the man.

He was wearing a headset and a name tag that said Tom for crying out loud. "I go to a lot of weddings. I'm at that age, you know? And men are always eager to get their name on my dance card if you get my meaning."

He furrowed his brow. "Unfortunately, yes."

Recognition dawned on her. "Are you Sydney's beau?"

He nodded. "You take any of her classes?"

"Yeah, I try to make the seven pm Sunday one on the regular. Yoga is a great way to set your intentions for the week ahead."

"I'll tell Sydney you said that." He flashed Daphne a friendly smile. "I'm sure she'll appreciate it." He gestured toward the door to the atrium. "Tabitha's ready for you. Go through here and out the side door. You luckily get the good stuff while the rest of the guests are suffering through passed apps and waiting out picture time."

"That is lucky." Daphne's stomach growled in anticipation. Maryann had mentioned Luis was working tonight. "Can I sneak you something?"

He grinned. "Nah, I can't eat on the job. Besides, Sydney's got some vegan nonsense waiting for me at home." He rolled his eyes. "We're doing a thirty-day meatless challenge. I don't recommend it. Longest thirty days of my life."

Daphne patted his arm and moved past him to the door. "I'll have some carnitas for you."

&.

TABITHA WAS out on the heated patio, standing in front of the taco truck chatting up Amos and Luis through the serving window, when Amos' eyes went wide. "Whoa," he said, slapping Luis on the arm with the back of his hand then pointing over Tabitha's shoulder.

She turned, not having to wonder who would elicit that sort of reaction from Amos, who was in a happy, committed relationship with his girlfriend, Petra. Only someone as beautiful as Daphne could make heads turn.

Daphne laughed when they all looked at her with their mouths agape and strode toward them like she was on a catwalk.

She was a vision in a rose gold silk strapless floor-length gown and gold flowing kimono printed with iridescent blue-, green-, and rose-colored butterflies.

"It gets better," she said, also signing the words for Amos. Daphne pressed something behind her ear and her chic updo sparkled with fairy lights twinkling amongst the gold filigree butterfly pins crowning her head.

"Whoa," Amos said again, before signing at her like a madman.

She signed back with equal enthusiasm.

Tabitha was curious and impressed. She'd been friends with Amos since high school and her ASL abilities were trash. She'd always relied on his cochlear implant and lip-reading skills to carry the weight of their conversations. She looked to Luis to see if he knew what they were saying. He shrugged.

"Cómo estás, Daphne?" Luis asked, gesturing up and down at her outfit. "You look like an intergalactic goddess." He smiled at Tabitha. "The two of you together are," he brought his fingers to his lips, "an actual chef's kiss, no?"

Daphne took Tabitha's hands and held them up. "Let me get a good look at your 'fit." She whistled. "That cape is fire and the jumpsuit, it's like it was custom made for you."

"Another one of my granny's treasures," Tabitha said, twisting from side-to-side. "I added the cape."

"Can I take a photo?" Amos asked, already aiming his phone at them. "Petra made me promise to send her pics. Probably of my first gig with Luis and not of other foxy ladies, but you all are foxy friends, so she won't care."

"Oh, yeah," Tabitha said. "Petra worked at Secondhand Rose. That must be why you're so good at sign language."

Daphne nodded. "She taught everyone in the shop. It's so helpful."

"Say cheese!" Amos said.

Tabitha and Daphne put an arm around each other's waists and tilted their heads toward one another.

Tabitha smiled so hard her ears popped.

Amos snapped one photo. Then a second and a third. He turned his phone horizontal to get another angle.

"Amos," Tabitha whined.

Luis clapped his hands. "Okay, enough pictures. Let's eat. What can I get you? I have to claim the menu is limited so people don't go overboard with substitutions, but I have everything on hand to make whatever you want."

"I'm dying for a carnitas burrito," Tabitha said, stepping out of the pose. "And a strawberry Jarritos. Champagne is not my thing."

"Ooh, I'll have the same order," Daphne said.

"You're killing me, Tab," Tom said into her headset.

Tabitha laughed. "Sorry. You know I can't turn this thing off until the event is over."

His only reply was a loud sigh and some mumble grumbles about vegetables.

Amos popped the bottle caps off the strawberry sodas and handed them to the women while Luis wrapped up their burritos with lightning speed.

"Let's go sit at the table by the coat check," Tabitha said, nodding back inside the atrium. "I'd hate to drip burrito juice on the linens before the guests sit down."

They took their food from Luis and made their way inside, Daphne holding the door for Tabitha.

THIS WAS ALREADY the best date Daphne had been on in years and it had only just begun. Beautiful woman, free food, and a chill atmosphere. She'd have to come to the Botanical Garden more often, she'd forgotten how peaceful it was to be surrounded by plants. And it smelled amazing. Earthy, fresh, tropical, and green.

They sat down at the round café table by the coat check, simultaneously peeling back the foil from their burritos and taking a bite.

"So good," Daphne said.

Tabitha nodded, pointing to her headset and then making a slashing motion across her neck.

Daphne gave her a thumbs up. The chairs that had made up the audience seating for the ceremony had been rearranged around several large round fully kitted out tables and somehow magically brought into the space in the time she was outside getting her food.

"The event staff are stealthy," Daphne said. "This place went from ceremony to reception in the blink of an eye!"

Tabitha finished chewing and swallowed. "We've got the transition down to under five minutes. My crew is the best."

"Except for poor Brian," Daphne said, giggling.

"Don't feel too sorry for him. He's another board member's relative. He doesn't actually need to work."

"I wonder what that's like. I've had a retail job of some kind since I was sixteen and I dominated in babysitting before that." Daphne pretended to brush off her shoulders. "More babies sat than any other teenager in all of Bethany Village."

"You grew up in Bethany?" Tabitha asked. "My first girlfriend went to Westview. We met at basketball camp."

Daphne set her burrito down and took a swig of her soda. "I went to Westview. I wonder if I know her?"

"Kaitlyn Oldson? Curly blond hair?"

Daphne choked on her drink. "She was my first kiss! Outdoor school in sixth grade."

"Wild," Tabitha said. "Your first kiss was in the sixth grade? When I was twelve, I didn't even know I liked girls yet. I was sure I was gonna marry Justin Bieber."

Daphne shrugged. "To each their own. I thought I was bi for a while because of Harry Styles. Some boys be pretty." She laughed and took a monster bite out of her burrito.

Tabitha gestured to the wide-open space between the reception tables. "Do you like to dance? The DJ we hired is new to us, but he's supposed to be great. He works with the couples to make custom playlists."

"Very cool," Daphne said. "I do love to dance even though I'm not great at it." She smiled, thinking about the last time she'd danced at a wedding. She hadn't meant to step on that drunk groomsman's toes. In her defense, who goes barefoot at a wedding in an art gallery? "My default is The Robot with a few ironic dabs tossed in for distraction."

Tabitha raised her eyebrows and a smirk spread across her lips. "This I have to see."

DAPHNE HADN'T LIED when she said she wasn't a great dancer, but the phrase that came to Tabitha's mind as she watched her date bringing her arms up to her forehead was *charmingly bad.*

Daphne finished dabbing to the funky disco beat the DJ was spinning and shimmied toward Tabitha.

"I told you." She laughed and took Tabitha's hands in hers, swinging them back and forth between them. "But this beat is sick. Keep this dude on the payroll."

Tabitha swayed her body to the music, drawing Daphne toward her and then pushing her away. "For sure."

When a slow song came on, instead of wrapping her arms around Daphne's waist like she wanted to, she froze. No one batted an eye at two women holding hands and dancing to fast music together but embracing Daphne here on this dance floor gave her pause. If anyone disapproved of same sex couples and complained to her boss, she could lose her job.

"Want to get another Jarritos?" Daphne asked, fanning her face with her hand. "I'm parched."

Tabitha nodded and followed Daphne out to the heated patio.

"For what it's worth," Daphne said over her shoulder, her voice low. "I can read a room and I don't think anyone would've cared if we'd slow danced. Even the older crowd seems pretty groovy." She dabbed as she drawled out the double o's in groovy.

"I'm being paranoid, I know," Tabitha said. "It's just, you're my first plus one at a work event. And I'm paying you for assisting me *before* the wedding but wanting to slow dance with you *at* the wedding. It's confusing."

Daphne grinned. "Beginnings always are, aren't they? But they're exciting too."

Amos was already popping the bottle caps off their sodas when they made it to the serving window. "Daph, I couldn't tell if you were dancing or trying to sign distress signals at me."

She took the drinks from him, screwing up her mouth. "I'm not completely sure either."

"Tabitha, you've got the moves," Luis said, one hand flat on his stomach and one raised as he Cha-Cha-ed the length of the mobile kitchen. "We should take a turn together."

"Twenty minutes until send-off," Tom's voice spoke into her ear.

Already? She'd lost track of time. "Copy

that," Tabitha said. She looked up at Luis. "I'll take a rain check on that dance. You can start tearing down now."

"Us too?" Daphne asked.

"Soon, but first can you help me pass out the send-off sparklers?"

Daphne squealed. "You just said my new favorite sentence."

THE NEWLYWED COUPLE walked hand-in-hand down the path that led to a white Bentley waiting at the curb, their way lit by the white and gold sparklers their friends and families held.

"I've never really thought about what sort of wedding I'd like to have," Daphne said, leaning in so Tabitha could hear her over the goodbyes, "but now I'm trying to figure out how to have sparklers going throughout the entire thing. And how to be outside in the winter for several hours. The way the light plays on the barren trees is gorgeous."

Tabitha looked away from the guests and toward the trees. "I love the way you see things, Daphne."

As the Bentley drove away, they stood inside the doors to the garden lobby each with a pail of water to collect everyone's spent sparklers. After the guests grabbed their coats and purses and retrieved their favor bags from their assigned tables, Daphne disassembled the arch while Tabitha helped the caterers with the linens and centerpieces.

What had taken a couple hours to set up came down in forty minutes. Daphne collected all the arch's component parts, stowing the lights, moss, and floral wire in a bin Tabitha had given her. She had no idea what to do with all the flowers and greenery. It seemed a shame to toss them in the trash. Maybe there was a compost pile?

"You can take some home if you want," Tabitha said. "Sometimes the bride or the families want them, but this one didn't."

"Thanks, I will," Daphne said, holding up the egg yolk yellow roses. "These are too pretty. The yellow is so vibrant." She began gathering them into a bouquet. "Hey, I hate to ask, but do you have a car here? I could use a ride home."

"Of course," Tabitha said. "I should've

offered earlier." She tucked a bright orange poppy behind her ear. "I was more focused on getting you here, I guess."

Daphne smiled. "Same. I usually take the bus, but I didn't even think about taking it home at this time of night dressed like this and carrying a mega bouq of roses. Normally I don't mind drawing attention to myself –"

"You've drawn mine for a while now," Tabitha blurted and then covered her mouth with her hand.

"Again, same. I should've asked you out ages ago. I wasn't sure you were into women, but I was sure you weren't the kind of person who would be mad if I'd guessed wrong. And now we're going to work together at least one more time. So, I mean, it's confusing and complicated," Daphne shrugged, "but I'm in if you are. I don't want to wait until the next wedding to see you again."

Tabitha lowered her hand from her mouth to her heart. "Sunday and Monday are my days off. Either of those work for you?"

"Either. Both," Daphne said.

Tabitha cackled and pointed to her headset. "Tom says we're adorable and we should go to Sydney's yoga class tomorrow evening. You like to set your intentions for the week there?"

"I do," Daphne said and then chuckled. There was fast, lesbian fast, and oh my gosh I just said 'I do' while holding a bouquet and standing across from a girl I like at the top of an aisle fast.

Tabitha was nice enough not to call her out. "Go ahead and leave the rest of the stuff there. My team will make sure everything gets put back where it belongs." She linked her arm with Daphne's. "Tell me all about our date tomorrow. I've never done yoga, although I do own four pairs of yoga pants."

"You're off to a great start then," Daphne said. "How are you at standing on one foot?"

Tabitha squeezed her arm. "I've got intermediate skills."

4

TABITHA ZIPPED up a soft pink fleece over her black tank top and looked at herself in the full-length mirror hanging on the back of her bedroom door. She'd tried on all four pairs of yoga pants and while they were all the same size, color, and cut, they were all different brands, and all fit her differently.

She sometimes envied her fellow lesbians who were into wearing men's clothes. Men's sizing was standard and based on measurements, on fact, not fictional numbers that companies had made up.

She'd decided on pair number three because her rear end looked the best in them. Pair number one was getting donated. There was some weird drooping going on in the fabric around her knees. Two and four went back in her dresser drawer in case Daphne wanted to take more yoga classes before Tabitha had a chance to do laundry.

Her phone rang on her bed and Tabitha flopped down next to it. She had no doubt it was Petra Facetiming, wanting all the deets that Amos had left out about the Daphne date. Tabitha had only known Petra for a year, but they'd become fast friends soon after Petra and Amos started dating.

Tabitha answered the call, rolling onto her back and holding the phone up above her face. "What's good?"

Petra smirked. "I'm hoping the story behind the pics of you and Daphne at that wedding last night. I've been nagging Amos to set the two of you up forever, but you know our track record with blind dates is awful. We might have redeemed ourselves and you two would be a power couple already."

Tabitha rolled her eyes. "It was one work date. The wedding won't be for six months at a minimum," she joked. The image of Daphne standing where the flower arch had been holding the bouquet of yellow roses and saying 'I do' popped into Tabitha's head.

Petra snorted. "Well, you two certainly look like you belong together. So gorgeous and glowing. Did Belle help Daph with her get up?"

"She didn't say. She nailed the Bohemian Formal theme though."

"You both did. I'm loving that cape on you. Amos and I created a sign for intergalactic goddess." She grinned. "It loosely translates to planetary Aphrodite."

"Ha! Perfect. Hey, did Amos tell you what he and Daphne were signing about? Luis and I were clueless. I may finally have to take an ASL class. I felt like a jerk not knowing what my oldest friend and my newest crush were saying to each other."

Petra shook her head. "He didn't mention anything." Her eyes lit up. "Maybe they were discussing a Valentine's Day surprise for me. You know we're about to have our first anniversary."

"That's probably it," Tabitha said. "And it makes sense he wouldn't want me to know since I'm awful at keeping secrets."

"Truth. So, when are you seeing Daphne again?"

Tabitha scanned the phone over her outfit. "We're going to a yoga class tonight."

"Fun," Petra drawled. "Although not many chances to talk."

"Yeah, I was thinking of asking her back here for a cup of tea." Tabitha twisted up her mouth. "Too forward? It's just that most places are closed at nine on a Sunday night."

"I'm not the person to ask when it comes to that. I kissed Amos, like, five hours after meeting him."

"Sure, but the two of you are the most spontaneous people I know. First date kissing is your vibe."

"Maybe your vibe is second date kissing?" Petra teased.

Tabitha's face heated. "Historically, I'm a third date quick goodbye kisser, but it's been a long time since I've had a third date. Work always gets in the way. Which I've been fine with. I love my job."

"Then it's perfect that Daphne is someone who can work and not work with you. I was going to say play, but that makes you sound like toddlers."

The women laughed. Tabitha shook her head. "I better go. I've got errands to run that I put off all week."

"Alrighty, have fun tonight. I think tea at your place is a lovely way to end a second date. And it will give you time to plan your third quick goodbye kiss date."

"I'm ending the call," Tabitha said, chuckling.

❧

DAPHNE CLIMBED down from the ladder where she'd been finishing up the lighting display in the Secondhand Rose front window. The instant her foot touched the ground, Belle rushed over.

"I've been waiting until I wouldn't distract you," Belle said. "I'm dying to know how your evening was."

Belle had come to work later than Daphne and as Daphne had already endured a lengthy chat about last night with Maryann, including comparing her insights with what Luis noted, she wanted to keep this brief.

"It was a wonderful time. Everyone loved

my 'fit and thought the light up hair was awesome. Tabitha and I ate yummy dinner and fast danced. I like her. We're going to yoga tonight."

Belle's shoulders slumped. "Maryann already got to you, didn't she? I wanted to be the one to dissect your date with you. Dang it!"

Daphne smirked. "You get dibs on first dish after yoga tonight, okay?"

"Fine," Belle said. "But how much excitement can happen during a yoga class?"

"She's invited me to have tea at her place after." Daphne folded up the ladder.

"Yoga and then tea? How very middle-aged of you." Belle grabbed a carved wooden cane nearby and offered it to Daphne.

Daphne rolled her eyes and headed toward the back with the ladder. "Well, we can't have coffee that late in the evening. No point in getting wired after spending an hour and a half destressing. Besides, I like tea and I think it's darling that she does too."

"It is darling," Belle said, breaking into a tap dance routine utilizing the cane. "And super middle-aged."

Daphne stored the ladder in the closet

next to Maryann's office. "Watch it, Belle, or I'll revoke your dibs."

Belle curved the hook at the top of the cane around her waist and mimed dragging herself down the men's leisure wear aisle.

§

TABITHA WALKED INTO BRAVEHEART YOGA. The lobby was filled with beautiful purple-green leafed plants hanging everywhere. Sydney, the owner, smiled at her from behind the front counter where she was checking people in.

"Daphne's not here yet, Tab," Sydney said around the blond woman in line in front of Tabitha.

The woman turned and gave her a slight smile that didn't cause movement anywhere else on her placid face. "Tab as in Tabitha?" she asked, extending her hand, a large diamond wedding band on her ring finger. "Lydia Cromwell. My husband, Matthew, is on the board at the Botanical Garden."

Tabitha nodded and politely shook Lydia's hand. "Nice to meet you."

It wasn't. Not at all. This had to be the woman who wanted her job.

Lydia didn't say it was nice to meet her, instead she gave her another one of those small, fake smiles. "Your event work is so youthful. Quite different from your former boss, Victorine."

Victorine had moved to Ashland down in Southern Oregon to run events for the Shakespeare Festival.

"Vic was wonderful to work for," Tabitha said, meaning it. "I'm grateful for everything she taught me. I'm just trying to bring my own style to the work, building from the strong foundation she left for me."

"Uh huh," Lydia said. Again, with that gross smile. She opened her mouth to give Tabitha another backhanded compliment.

"You're all checked in, Lydia," Sydney said, thrusting the woman's punch card at her.

Lydia snatched it from Sydney's hand. "Enjoy the class," she said to Tabitha, her eyes narrowing. "Oh, look, here's Daphne."

"Lydia," Daphne said.

"I saw the new window display at Secondhand Rose." She brushed some nonexistent lint from her navy blue cashmere sweater, looking away from Daphne. "It's quite eclectic."

"I aim to confuse," Daphne said, dismissing her and turning toward Tabitha. "Hey, there." She put her hand on Tabitha's lower back and nudged her forward, edging Lydia out of line.

Sydney handed Tabitha a fresh punch card with one class punched out. "Your first class is on the house," she said. "And if you think you're going to become a regular, I can get you set up with an account and you can scan yourself in with a plastic member card like Daphne has."

"Cool, thank you," Tabitha said, taking the card from Sydney. She lowered her voice. "Is Lydia a regular?" Tabitha couldn't help but think she was being spied on. She stepped away from Daphne's touch.

Daphne slid her card underneath the scanner mounted on the edge of the counter. "She comes in about once a month. Why?"

"I think she's the person who wants my job," Tabitha said.

"Funny, this is her second Sunday in a

row," Daphne said, her brows pinching together.

Sydney sighed and shook her arms out. "Let's not read too much into this, ladies. Maybe her trip to Cabo got canceled." She strode into the studio, motioning for them to follow her.

It was too much of a coincidence. No, Braverton wasn't a huge place and people ran into each other all the time everywhere, but Lydia had shown up to yoga with freshly blown out hair, wearing full make-up, a cashmere sweater, and ballet flats. The burgundy-colored leggings were the only aspect of her outfit that seemed appropriate.

Daphne took her hand, pulling her toward the studio.

Tabitha slid her hand out of Daphne's grip. "I don't think I can do this. She's trying to dig up dirt on me."

"And I'm dirt?" Daphne huffed.

"You know what I mean," Tabitha said, her gaze pleading with Daphne not to be offended. "She'll be able to tell we're not just friends."

"Is there some sort of clause in your contract that the event planner at the garden can't be a lesbian?" Daphne asked, crossing her arms.

"No, of course not. But if word gets around that we're dating and I hired you to work for me," her shoulders slumped and she exhaled hard through her nose, "that doesn't look good."

"Okay, then I won't work for you again. It was a one-time emergency." Daphne shrugged. "Can we go in now? I think we need it more than ever."

Tabitha scrubbed at her eyes with her fingertips. "But I need you on the next job. Brian won't be ready. And I've got a huge benefit on Valentine's Day that could use your expertise."

"So, I guess the real question is," Daphne said, stepping back from Tabitha. "Do you want to date me or work with me?"

Tabitha pressed her lips together. "You know I wish it could be both, but I've worked too hard to get where I'm at in my career to throw it away on a relationship that has barely just begun."

"Wow. Okay. I get it," Daphne said, shaking her head like she most definitely didn't get it. "See you next Saturday." She turned and walked into the yoga studio, closing the door behind her.

Stunned, Tabitha stood gawking at the door for a moment before leaving Braveheart Yoga and heading to her car. She pictured the small table in her kitchen she'd covered with a bright floral tablecloth, on which she had set out a plate of Madeleines and two white porcelain teacups rimmed with a silver stripe. All she would have to do was boil water and they could sit down to a lovely tea for two.

Tears welled in her eyes, and she swiped them away with the cuff of her fleece. What was she so afraid of? If Lydia stole her job, then wouldn't Lydia have the same conflict of interest that Tabitha had? And what about Brian? He had a family connection at the garden.

But because she was young, and Black, and a woman who liked women, the rules were different for her than for all the older, privileged white people who made up the majority of the board and staff at the garden. Being Korean, being gay, she'd thought Daphne would identify with the extra hoops she had to jump through. Know what being in the minority was like. Maybe she did and she didn't care. Maybe Daphne was braver than she was.

Tabitha unlocked her car and sat in the driver's seat, taking in deep breaths and breathing out slowly.

"This is stupid," she said out loud. "I'm being stupid. I'm not letting that mean lady win!"

Tabitha got out of her car and walked back to Braveheart. The door was locked, so she knocked on the window until Sydney came out of the studio, the annoyance on her face changing to surprise when she saw who was interrupting her class.

"We're doing some light stretching and deep breathing," Sydney said after letting Tabitha in. "Grab a mat from the basket by the door and find a spot. I'm glad you decided to join us after all."

The entire class twisted to look at her as she walked in. Tabitha chose a mat and laid it out right next to Daphne's.

She sat cross-legged on her mat like everyone else was doing, resting her hands on her knees, palms up. "I'm an idiot," Tabitha whispered to Daphne.

Daphne reached over and put her hand on top of Tabitha's, squeezing it once, twice. "Shh. We're silently setting our intentions for the week."

She closed her eyes, so Tabitha followed along and closed hers too, thinking her intention for the week was to see Daphne every day.

5

DAPHNE MET Amos at the backdoor of the Pinwheel Plant Shop. Although he was in school full-time to become a librarian, he still worked, like, eight different gigs. Delivering plants for Avery, the owner of the plant shop, was one of them.

Later she would head to the garden to set up for that evening's wedding, but first she and Amos had some good-natured scheming to do.

"Did you bring the stuff I asked you to?" Daphne signed.

Amos pushed a bin full of decorations toward her with his foot. "Ta-da," he said, doing jazz hands.

"Cool," she signed. "I'm going to stow this in Jade's office at the Cask and Goblet. I can't believe you rented the whole place out on Valentine's Day. That must have cost a fortune."

"Why do you think I picked up another gig with Luis?" Amos signed. "I want this to be momentous. Epic!" He shrugged. "Jade gave me a good rate. She took pity on a poor graduate student."

"You still want me to keep this a secret from Tabitha?" Daphne signed. She bent to pick up the bin, happy she didn't have to go far. It weighed a ton.

"Please," Amos said. "Tabitha is a blabbermouth."

Daphne laughed.

"How's that going?" Amos asked. "You two?"

She crinkled up her nose and set the bin on her knee to reposition her hands. "It's going awesome. We've seen each other every day since last Saturday." Daphne grinned. "I've never drank so much tea in my life." Or restrained herself from kissing someone for so long. She wasn't sure what they were waiting for, but neither one of them had made a move.

Amos smiled. "I'm happy for you."

Avery poked her head out the back door of the shop. "There you are, Amos." She nodded at Daphne. "I've got a Dieffenbachia that needs to go to Braverton Christian Church before three. They just called. Not the plant I would choose for a memorial service, but no one asked me."

"Talk to you later, Daph," Amos said.

"Later." Daphne hauled the bin through the parking lot and across the street. She lightly tapped the toe of her foot on the front door of the Cask and Goblet to get the owner's attention. Jade hurried around the bar and unlocked the door, holding it open for her.

"Come in, come in," Jade said, rushing past Daphne toward the storage closet. "You can set that on the floor here."

Daphne slid the bin into the closet and shook out her arms. "I've got my work cut out for me. I think there's seven million strands of lights in there."

Jade clasp her hands under her chin. "Ah,

but it's going to be so romantic. *J'adore l'amour.*" She sighed.

"*Moi aussi,*" Daphne said, shutting the door. "And now I'm off to my next adventure. Still okay for me to get started around four on V Day?"

"Yes, I'll need to be in the kitchen, but will help as much as I can."

Daphne gave her a thumbs up and headed to the back door. "See you later."

She walked to the Botanical Garden, her hands deep in the pockets of her swing coat and her chin tucked into the collar. The weather was typical February; cloudy with the temperature nearing fifty but so windy it felt like thirty.

Daphne went over her plans for that night's lighting in her head. As far as she knew, Brian hadn't planned anything, so this design would truly be her own.

The theme was, "Sunset in Tahiti," which was way more obvious than the theme of the last wedding. She was going to use lots of red, orange, and blue lights around the arch and had the inkling of an idea about increasing the brightness of the starlight overhead as the overall mood lighting grew darker blue.

She smiled into the collar of her coat thinking about how Tabitha had reacted to her idea. "That sounds amazing. But how?" she'd asked. Daphne had shrugged and said, "Art finds a way." She'd known it would rile her a little. Daphne was learning she liked it when Tabitha got a bit feisty.

After their argument at yoga on Sunday and Tabitha's brave return, Daphne realized they would need to go more slowly than she was used to. Which was okay. Tabitha had more than proven herself worth the wait over the past week.

So, the war was within. Daphne against Daphne. What she wanted and what Tabitha needed. A kiss would come when Tabitha was ready.

Tom met her at the door of the lobby to let her in. "Welcome back," he said.

"Glad to be back," Daphne said.

"Tab's in the atrium."

Daphne strode toward the event space, taking off her coat as she walked, and dropping it on an aisle seat in the last row.

The frame of the arch was already assembled and adorned with white and yellow hibiscus. It was flanked on either side by huge arrangements of tropical plants.

"Hey," Tabitha said from the coat check, where she was setting up a table. "The 40-foot ladder you asked for should be here in a few. We had to get it out of storage. The garden installation team only uses it twice a year, I guess."

Daphne rubbed her hands together. "Great. I'll start on the arch and save the sky for last. Give the idea time to marinate in the old noggin."

"I don't know how you can be so calm not knowing," Tabitha said, finishing up with the table. "I'm having a panic attack on your behalf."

"Aw, don't freak out," Daphne said, approaching Tabitha and taking hold of her shoulders. "I'm ninety-two percent certain."

Tabitha brought her hands up and put them on top of Daphne's. "Okay, that's slightly more reassuring."

They stood facing one another, staring into each other's eyes for a long moment. Daphne fought against taking a step closer and moving her hands from Tabitha's shoulders down her arms and pulling her into an embrace. Pressing her lips to Tabitha's, feeling the softness of her lush mouth.

Instead, Tabitha used that beautiful mouth of hers to flash Daphne a bright smile, one that seemed to promise, "Not here, not now, but soon."

Daphne reluctantly withdrew her hands from underneath Tabitha's. "That arch isn't going to light itself."

"But somehow you still seem to make magic," Tabitha said, her voice low.

§

SHE LAY next to Daphne on the tile floor of the atrium, smack dab in the middle of the aisle, looking up.

Gauzy, foot-wide strips of deep blue and purple fabric strung across the atrium ceiling at two-foot intervals. The rising moon shone like a spotlight on the fabric, which Daphne had hole-punched in a random pattern to look like a smattering of stars.

The combination of the real sky and Daphne's creation was breathtaking and would be even more so when the moon was right above the atrium ceiling.

"I love your brain," Tabitha said, scooting her head over so it rested against Daphne's shoulder. "It's so weird and wonderful."

Daphne pushed a button on a small remote clenched in her hand. "Check this out."

The soft yellow standard overhead lighting morphed into a cooler blue color while the ombre layered bulbs on the arch mimicked a sunset over the ocean.

"If the people who hold daytime weddings here knew what the nighttime people got for the identical price," Tabitha said. She rolled onto her side at the same time Daphne did, facing each other.

"I'm trying with all my might to go slow, Tabitha," Daphne said, "but you are the most kissable person in all the land."

Tabitha bit the inside of her lip. She'd caught Daphne looking at her mouth more than once over the past week. She knew what Daphne wanted and Tabitha wanted it too. She propped herself up on her elbow, nearing Daphne, silently nudging her onto her back, Tabitha's eyes roaming over the woman's little rosebud lips.

Tabitha cupped Daphne's face with her

free hand and captured her mouth in a sweet, tentative kiss.

Daphne's hand went to the back of Tabitha's neck, pulling her closer, deepening the kiss.

Tom cleared his throat. "Tabitha. Daphne."

The women smiled against each other's mouths. "We've been caught," Daphne whispered.

Another throat clearing. This time from a more feminine voice.

Tabitha's heart stopped, fear shooting through her. She was on her feet in an instant. Smoothing the front of her skirt.

Daphne stood next to her. Too close. Tabitha hated herself for it, but she stepped away.

"Oops," Daphne said. "Please excuse us. We were caught up in a moment."

"Clearly," the bride, Angelica, said. Her face set in fury.

Tom gave Tabitha a look that asked, "Want me to stay when this all goes sideways?"

She gave him a barely perceptible shake

of her head. She was a big girl and she'd messed up.

"Where are the tiki torches?" Angelica asked, scowling at the arch. As her stare went from the altar to the atrium ceiling, her jaw clenched. "Why is the glass ceiling covered up with hippie tapestries? The whole point of getting married here is that you can see the sky."

Tom made to leave, but Angelica grabbed his arm. "Can you see the sky?"

"Um, yeah, I can. In between the fabric."

Angelica rolled her eyes so hard that Tabitha thought she might have lodged them in her brain. "That was a rhetorical question," she ground out.

Tom removed her hand from his arm and backed toward the lobby door.

"There were supposed to be tiki torches?" Daphne asked behind Tabitha.

"What else would you have at a Tahitian Sunset themed wedding?" Angelica spat.

Tabitha started to speak, to diffuse this situation.

"Um, a sunset," Daphne said, coming up to stand next to Tabitha like she was making a united front. She pointed to the ceiling. "A night sky like you might see in Tahiti. The actual ceiling is serving Braverton sky, not Tahitian. I still let it shine through because I wanted to play with the idea this is all a fantasy created within reality."

"Well, it's stupid and I want it taken down immediately," Angelica said, training her glare on Tabitha. "Are you going to say anything or just let your rude girlfriend do all the talking? Where's Brian? Brian sold me on tiki torches, and I want tiki torches."

"Brian had an accident. He fell off a ladder." She sounded like a ten-year-old who'd been caught sneaking money from her mother's purse. "And not that it's an excuse, but he didn't give me any lighting plans for your event."

"Is it not your job to manage all aspects of the weddings here?" Angelica asked, taking her phone out of her purse. She began snapping photos. "Or were you too busy thinking about swapping spit with Miss Artsy Fartsy?" She shook her head. "You're both so fired."

Daphne rushed toward Angelica and put her hand over the phone's camera. "Chill.

We will take it down and do exactly what you want. There's no need to make threats."

Tabitha cringed. Never, ever, ever tell a bride to chill. "Daphne, please get started on the take down."

Angelica swatted Daphne's hand away from her phone. "You want me to chill? How's this for chill?" She looked around Daphne, her eyes locking on Tabitha's. "The wedding is off. I'll take my business some-where where they appreciate their clients."

"You can't do that," Daphne said, lightly grabbing Angelica's arm. "This has gone sideways. I promise we can fix–"

"Get your hand off of me," Angelica said.

Tabitha hastily put her headset on. "Tom, we've got a situation."

Daphne stepped away from Angelica with her hands up, shooting Tabitha a con-fused and hurt look. "There's no situation. Should I just go?"

Tabitha nodded, looking away from Daphne. Best, worst, and most memorable first kiss ever and for all the wrong reasons. "Sorry," she mumbled.

Tom walked through the door, his face

puzzled as Daphne grabbed her coat and bag and rushed past him out the door.

Angelica snorted. "I don't know why you're apologizing to her. I'm the one with a ruined wedding venue."

Tabitha had half a mind to quit and run after Daphne, but her rent was due on the 15th and she couldn't pay it with warm fuzzy feelings. So, she set her jaw.

"Angelica, what do I have to do to make this right?"

"Get me my tiki torches and we'll go from there." She turned and left the room in a huff.

"How can I help?" Tom asked.

Tabitha gestured to the ceiling. "Are you afraid of heights?"

Tom shook his head.

"This all needs to come down."

6

DAPHNE HURRIED toward the bus stop, swiping at the tears on her cheeks with the sleeve of her coat. She'd never felt so led astray in her life. Tabitha had gone from being self-assured and capable one minute to practically begging at that bridezilla's feet.

Yes, Tabitha's job was on the line, but any reasonable person would've spoken up for themselves. Daphne had, although she knew she'd come off a little art snobbish. She'd been defensive because her heart was still basking in the sunshine of Tabitha's compliments and that kiss.

That perfect, cinematic, weak in the knees making first kiss.

Tabitha was going to text her later, explaining herself. Give Daphne a real apology. She felt sure of it. After all the lead up and back and forth, Tabitha wasn't going to bail on her.

Right?

Daphne leaned against the outside wall of the blue bus stop shelter and rummaged through her bag for her bus pass. She drew in a calming breath. Today was a bump on their path to a real relationship. She was confident they could recover.

❧

SITTING ON HER BED, nursing her third cup of tea, Daphne glanced at her phone. The wedding would've started by now, that is if the bridezilla had been bluffing. She imagined that was the case. It would be too much trouble to actually cancel a wedding only four hours before guests were supposed to arrive.

Right?

Tabitha was probably too stressed to text her yet and waiting until the ordeal was through before getting in touch. Daphne set the cold tea aside and scooted down into her covers, glancing at the flowy orange slip dress hanging from the top of her closet door. She'd planned on wearing it to the wedding tonight before everything became such a hot mess.

DAPHNE AWOKE. The sky outside her bedroom window was pitch black and the busy street that ran in front of her duplex was silent. She searched in her twisted-up blankets for her phone, finding it stashed underneath her pillow. It was three o'clock in the morning. She swiped her thumb up the home screen.

No texts.

No missed calls.

Maybe Tabitha hadn't wanted to wake her. Maybe Tabitha had been exhausted and crabby and not in the right frame of mind to talk. Daphne could accept that.

Well, if that was the case.

It was possible Tabitha was blowing her off. Maybe she thought Daphne was in the wrong? If that was the way she felt, Tabitha could stay gone. Daphne was not about to text her. Not when Tabitha was clearly in the wrong.

Right?

She set her phone on her bedside table and turned off the lamp, tears threatening to spill from her eyes once more.

They were supposed to go to yoga tomorrow night. If Tabitha didn't show up, Daphne would have her answer, wouldn't she?

DAPHNE PUSHED OPEN the door to Braveheart Yoga, crossing her fingers that Tabitha would be there. She'd gotten to class before Daphne last week, but it wasn't a given she'd be early this week.

Sydney met Daphne's eyes as she got in line to scan her card. After the person in front of Daphne headed into the studio, Sydney glanced around to make sure no one else was within earshot.

"Have you talked to Tabitha?" Sydney asked, her voice low.

Daphne shook her head. "No, I've been waiting for her to get in touch with me."

Sydney cringed. "She's probably spiraling pretty bad, considering."

"Was the wedding a disaster or what?" Daphne sort of hoped that it was because that's what bridezilla deserved, but for Tabitha's sake, she didn't want it to be a total flop.

"Oh, there was no wedding," Sydney said. "Tom and Tab took all your work down and did exactly as that..." Sydney took a deep cleansing breath, "woman requested and then when the ceremony was set to start, the bride asked everyone to reconvene over at the Elks Lodge because there was no way she was going to let the gardens swindle her out of her dream wedding."

Daphne ground her teeth. "No."

"Yes," Sydney said. "The board is sure to fire Tabitha now."

"No," Daphne said again. "The bride was in the wrong. She was being totally unreasonable."

Sydney frowned sympathetically. "I agree, but Tom seems to think you riled bridezilla up."

Daphne put her face in her hands. "I did. She deserved it, though. I wish Tabitha had stood up for herself, for me. We were being bullied and threatened."

"Well, it sounds to me like Tabitha wishes you'd sucked it up and kept your mouth shut." Sydney put her hand on Daphne's. "I know it's difficult to deal with people like that. Unfortunately, it's the price we pay for working with the public."

"Boo to the public," Daphne said.

"C'mon. Let's go do class, get centered, and then I'll help you figure out what you're going to say when you call Tab after."

Daphne nodded, dropping her shoulders. This was still just a bump. An Everest-sized bump, but she was a good climber.

7

___

Tabitha lay on the beige carpeted floor of her family room dressed in the good yoga pants and a pale yellow fitted tank top. She should be at yoga.

Ascribing to the idea that you dress for success, Tabitha had put on workout clothes in the hopes that they would somehow magically make her want to do yoga.

Alas, it hadn't done the trick this time.

Instead, she was sprawled on the floor, staring at the popcorn ceiling, and consuming her weight in gummy worms.

Chewing was a form of exercise. Maybe it also released some endorphins?

"C'mon endorphins," she muttered to herself, "any time now."

Seeing Daphne would've made her feel better even though she was still a tiny bit mad at her for antagonizing Angelica. But, as it turned out, Angelica was worthy of Daphne's ire and then some.

All that work she and poor Tom had put into making things just as that bridezilla wanted and it was all for nothing.

How could she face Daphne knowing that her unemployment was imminent? That she had no idea how to be a real adult, that she had failed, and would have to move back in with her parents?

Okay, she had enough money for this month's rent, but next month was a definite no.

Her phone rang and she picked it up off her stomach.

The number for the Botanical Garden office appeared on the screen.

She sat up, finished chewing the gummies in her mouth, and answered the call.

"Hello, this is Tabitha," she said, mustering up her professional voice.

"Hello, dear. This is Miranda Rutledge."

Tabitha bit her tongue. How had she thought she'd ever make it at the gardens when everyone in charge spoke to her like she was their sweet little granddaughter? She'd been so naïve.

"I'll cut to the chase, if you don't mind. I know it's your day off and that you worked your hiney off last night despite the wedding being canceled."

Mrs. Rutledge cleared her throat and Tabitha could practically hear her glaring at someone. It gave her a small satisfaction. Not everyone on the board hated her.

"I'm ready," Tabitha said, biting off the head of a gummy. If she was getting canned, what did it matter if they could hear her chewing.

"After a vote of seven to five, I'm afraid that we will have to terminate your employment with the Braverton Botanical Garden effective one week from today, on the thirteenth. Perhaps gain a few more years of experience and we would love to have you back."

"I don't know what to say," Tabitha said. "Well, I guess I do. I had hoped this wouldn't be the outcome and that the board would offer me some grace. I have, as you said, worked my hiney off for the garden."

"I know dear," Mrs. Rutledge said, lowering her voice. "And five of us were happy for you to stay."

"Tell her about the Valentine's Day event, Miranda," a man's voice said in the background. "Let's get that locked in before we adjourn."

"I was getting to it, Cromwell. Hold your horses," Mrs. Rutledge said. "As you know, the Valentine's Day event is coming up. Lydia Cromwell has been elected, again by a vote of seven to five, as the interim events coordinator. She's asked that you assist her at the event as your final duty."

Tabitha nearly choked on her candy. "But I don't have to assist her if I don't want to, correct? My employment ends the day before the party."

"No, you don't," Mrs. Rutledge said. "And if I were you, I wouldn't."

"Miranda! For heaven's sake," Mr. Cromwell shouted in the background.

"But you're much nicer and not jaded like I am," Mrs. Rutledge quickly added.

Tabitha snorted. The Valentine's Day

event was a fundraiser, after all, and Mrs. R couldn't one hundred percent throw the garden under the bus. "Okay, I'll help out one last time as long as I am paid time and a half."

"That is very gracious of you, Tabitha. Double overtime, it is."

"Miranda," Mr. Cromwell growled.

"Thank you, Mrs. Rutledge," Tabitha said. "May I use you as a reference?"

"Of course, dear. Bye now."

"Goodbye." Tabitha ended the call and tossed her phone onto the carpet beside her and lay back down.

That hadn't been so bad. At least it was over. Mr. Cromwell was always going to get his way, no matter how well she'd done. That was the real failure here. A system that let rich, white people run things. She stuck her hand in the bag of gummy worms and took out a few, cramming them in her mouth.

Her phone rang again. When she saw it was Daphne calling, she swiped to answer the call as fast as she could.

"Daphne," she began.

"I'm sorry I have a big mouth," Daphne said, cutting her off. "I just couldn't take how disrespectful Angelica was. We both deserve better."

"And I'm sorry I momentarily lost my spine. It won't happen again. You're right. I deserve respect. No matter my age or skin color or income level. I'm a good person and was great at my job."

"Was?" Daphne asked. "Shoot."

"It's okay. Really," Tabitha said, kicking her feet up onto the couch. She gave her the rundown of the phone call with the board.

"Can I take you out to dinner tomorrow?" Daphne asked. "We can plan your next career move... and talk about where we're going too."

Tabitha grinned. "I can't wait to hear what your beautiful mind comes up with."

8

———————

DAPHNE SAT on the floor in the back corner of the Secondhand Rose, polishing a silver serving set. Although they kept it in a locked glass case, it still needed cleaning once a month. Daphne, not for the first time, wished someone would take the lovely set off their hands. Someone who was really into polishing tiny intricate roses that lined literally every single item.

The bell on the door rang and Daphne made to get up, but Belle whispered, "I got this," from over by the leather-bound books.

"Welcome in," Belle said. "Please let me know if there is anything I can assist you with."

"We're good, thanks," a woman said, her voice familiar.

Daphne heard them walk over to the sale rack. She stooped down to look underneath the clothing racks between them and her, thinking she might be able to figure out who they were from what shoes they were wearing.

Black Nike sneakers and green Clarks clogs did not jog her memory.

"What do you think of this?" the familiar voice said.

"Ooh, yes. That screams Tahiti to me, all the oranges and reds. Would you wear it out or as a cover up?"

"Hmm. The all-inclusive resort we're staying at is super laid back. It can work as both."

"I love an all-inclusive resort," the other woman said, chuckling. "Especially when you're not the one paying for it."

"I know," the familiar voice drawled. "I was kinda bummed at first that I had to move the wedding from the botanical garden to the Elks Lodge, but when I saw the upgrade your Auntie Lydia got us for the honeymoon, I knew I made the right choice."

Daphne bit the inside of her lip to keep herself from shouting.

Angelica.

Of course, she and Meanie Cromwell were in cahoots. Daphne knew Angelica was protesting way too much about things that could've been fixed. She'd never planned on having her wedding at the garden, no matter what happened.

Daphne knew confronting her would do no good and she didn't want to give Lydia Cromwell the satisfaction of knowing her plan had worked despite Daphne learning what had really gone down. Not to mention that Maryann wouldn't be too keen on a cat fight in the shop.

"I'm just gonna get this. I don't need to try it on," Angelica said.

"Cool," her friend, niece of Meanie Cromwell, said. "I got a ton of new stuff at Lululemon yesterday, so I'm good. Let's go grab a bubble tea."

Belle rang Angelica up. "Did I hear you say this was for your honeymoon?" Belle asked.

"Yes, Tahiti. We leave day after tomorrow."

"Aw, congratulations. I hope you have a wonderful time. I love Tahiti... but please tell me you're not staying at the La Maridia resort. I had the worst food poisoning of my life there."

"Um, yeah, that's where we're staying."

Daphne got to her knees and scooted over until she could see this encounter through the racks.

Belle giggled. "Oh, I'm sure it will be fine by now. They've probably disinfected everything. I don't suppose an e. coli outbreak can last forever."

Angelica took her bag from Belle, her shoulders slumped. "You got e. coli?"

"Yup. And salmonella. And giardia." Belle cringed. "Oh, and lockjaw."

"You're kidding me," Angelica said, shaking her head.

"I would never kid about lockjaw."

"Phone your aunt," Angelica said to her friend, grabbing her by the arm and nudging her through the front door.

"Congrats, again," Belle called, waving after them.

When the coast was clear, Daphne stood. "You know who that was, don't you?"

Belle rolled her eyes. "Yes. I thought the fear of constant runs during her honeymoon was what she deserved."

Daphne burst out laughing. "Thank you. That was clutch. You didn't really get lockjaw, did you?"

"Of course not. La Maridia is a lovely all-inclusive resort. The only one in Tahiti. Ten out of ten would visit again." Belle began hula dancing out from behind the counter.

Daphne joined in, meeting her by the jewelry case. "Now that you've meted out some justice to Angelica, I need to come up with an equally crafty way to give Lydia Cromwell what's coming to her."

"You'll think of something fantastic and weird," Belle said, hip-bumping her.

"Something that doesn't involve me opening up my big mouth."

"It would be funnier if you did," Belle sang.

"You are a champion pot stirrer, Belle Walden."

Belle broke from doing the hula and moved seamlessly into a stirring the pot motion.

Daphne shook her head and trudged

back to the silver. "Polishing will help me think."

❧

DAPHNE STRODE from the Braverton Print Shop next door to Small's, carrying a small brown paper bag.

Tabitha waved to her from a table in the middle of the restaurant seating area, the number stand on the table indicating she'd already ordered.

"I was gonna treat you," Daphne called.

Tabitha shrugged. "Get me a banana pudding?"

Daphne nodded and moved forward in line. She smiled to herself, glad that things between them seemed to be back to normal. Whatever that meant.

She stepped up to the counter. "I'll take a vegan sides plate with fried chicken, a Trixie's Ginger Beer, and two banana puddings."

The counter person opened and slid the ginger beer and a number stand to her while she paid. "I'll send the puddings out with your meal."

Daphne sat down across from Tabitha,

placing her drink and the brown paper bag on the table before shucking off her coat onto the top of the chair.

"What's in the bag?" Tabitha asked. "Something from the print shop?"

"Indeed, it is. Something for you." Daphne took a quick sip of her ginger beer and then opened the bag, taking out the box of four hundred business cards.

"For me?" Tabitha opened the box and took out a sunny yellow card. "Bright Smile Event Planning: Event Design that Shines." She raised an eyebrow at Daphne. "Black woman owned and operated. LGBTQIA+ and disability friendly. Eclectic. Youthful. Trend-forward." Tabitha rubbed her thumb across the embossing. "You got the high-end printing and paper for a business that doesn't exist?"

"But what if it did?" Daphne asked, reaching for Tabitha's free hand. "You're a woman of intermediate skills. Why can't you have your own event planning company?"

Tabitha chewed her bottom lip. "I'm not all these things it says I am, though."

"Aren't you though?" Daphne held up a finger for each item on the list. "Black.

Woman. Lesbian. Besties with a hard-of-hearing guy and his ASL interpreter girlfriend. You wear your granny's vintage clothes but add your own elements. Was there specialized lighting or taco trucks or custom playlists before you took over events at the garden?"

Tabitha ducked her head and shook it. "No."

"See? You're all those things and more. You'd be crazy not to strike out on your own, especially since so many people love and appreciate you and would be happy to help you build a business." Daphne wiped a tear from Tabitha's cheek with the pad of her thumb. "I believe in you."

Tabitha drew Daphne's hand to her lips and kissed it. "I knew you'd come up with something brilliant. How do you do it?"

"Honestly, I came up with this while I was polishing silver." Daphne scrunched up her nose. "I have something to tell you. It's the reason for phase two of your career plan."

She blanched. "Can we wait until pudding? I have a feeling I'm not going to love phase two."

A server brought over both of their meals – they'd ordered identical entrees – and the banana puddings.

Daphne dropped Tabitha's hand and dug into a banana pudding, nodding at Tabitha to do the same. "Dessert first."

"Oh, fine, just tell me." She took up the other pudding and scooped a huge bite into her mouth.

Daphne told her about Angelica's visit to the Secondhand Rose and what she had discovered.

Tabitha stabbed her spoon into her pudding.

"I understand the stabbiness, but I think handing out these snazzy business cards at the Valentine's Event, that is sure to be mediocre because Lydia is running it, is the classy way to exact your vengeance." Daphne giggled. "And Belle took care of ruining Angelica's honeymoon."

"Do I want to know?" Tabitha asked, finishing the dessert and moving on to her main course.

"Not while we're eating," Daphne said.

Tabitha cringed. "Gross. Okay, well now

that we've talked career plans, is there anything you want to say about us?"

Daphne stuffed a bite of black-eyed pea salad into her mouth. "You first."

Tabitha waved her hand over the business cards. "This right here is girlfriend-level meddling."

Daphne swallowed and took a long pull from her ginger beer. Tabitha's tone was neutral. Was girlfriend-level meddling a good thing or a bad thing? "And?" she asked.

Tabitha grinned widely at her. "So, I guess that makes you my girlfriend."

Daphne smiled back at her. Her teeth were probably full of kale slaw, but she didn't care. They'd summited the bump and were on their way to smooth terrain.

9

"THAT DOESN'T GO THERE," Lydia said from behind Tabitha.

Tabitha picked up the tall plaster urn full of floral foam and spray-painted moss and gestured with the toe of her shoe at the X marked in masking tape on the temporary stage floor. "You said to put this on the X didn't you?"

Lydia rolled her eyes at Tabitha like she must be dumb. "Not that X." She pointed to the other side of the stage where Tabitha was going to place a second, identical urn next. "There."

"These urns are the same. What does it matter which one gets set first?"

"Because it does, obviously," Lydia said, turning her back on Tabitha and heading over to a wheelchair-bound Brian who was directing one of the team members to tack a string of gold lights around a big vinyl cutout heart stuck to the wall.

There would be holes in the wall, but she supposed that wasn't her problem anymore.

Tabitha marched to the other side of the stage and set the ugly decoration down on the X. Whatever. She just needed to get through this night and then she would officially be her own boss.

The thought scared and excited her but knowing that Daphne would be by her side eased some of her anxiety.

Tabitha set the other urn and then moved on to the next item on the long list of duties Lydia had prepared for her.

JADE AND DAPHNE stood at the kitchen door, peeking into the dining room as Amos wiped his mouth with the red cloth napkin gripped tightly in his hand and then slid from his chair onto one knee beside the table. He held up an open black velvet box.

Petra gasped and put a hand on her chest. Behind her, framing the booth they were seated in, an arch of lights in the shape of roses sparkled in such a way that they appeared to be blooming. Beneath the arch were the words, "I love you," spelled out in red neon.

"Petra," Amos began, his voice shaky, "this last year with you has been the best of my life…"

"Should we be watching this?" Jade whispered.

"I'd rather see it live than on TikTok later," Daphne whispered back.

"*Quelle*?" Jade asked.

"Amos had me rig up a camera to record the proposal. It's hidden at the top of the O in love."

"So, we're not being terribly intrusive?"

Daphne gave a quiet snort. "We are, but people don't care about privacy anymore. Social media or it didn't happen."

Petra shouted, "Yes!" and then got down on her knees and dragged Amos into an excited hug. They stayed that way for a moment, laughing and crying and swaying back and forth before he finally got the ring on her finger.

Jade sighed, her hand on her heart. "Do you think they'll let me use stills from the video in my print ads?"

❧

TABITHA WEAVED her way through the crowded atrium, business cards in hand. Daphne had told her to be strategic about who she gave them to. Since the event was a fundraiser, the guests were older people with money to burn.

Was she aware of any attendees with kids who were near their age and recently engaged? Anyone with a special wedding anniversary coming up? Or a retirement? These people are the same people, Daphne pointed out. Also, she needed to be on the lookout for gay men of all ages as Daphne had attended two outdoor kitchen-warming parties last summer. Any excuse for a party.

She skirted the edge of the dance floor scanning for potential clients, trying to remember all of her girlfriend's advice.

Luis and Maryann waltzed toward her, Luis dramatically dipping Maryann when they got nearby.

"Thank you so much for the tickets," Maryann said as Luis drew her to him. They both held out their left hands, wedding bands on their ring fingers. "We hit up the courthouse earlier today and are now enjoying free food, drinks, and dancing, thanks to you. It's like our own little wedding reception."

"Except no family and friends to toast us," Luis lamented.

Maryann hugged him close. "Soon, my love."

Tabitha handed them her card. "Congratulations! I'd love to offer my services free of charge so you can have the reception of your dreams sooner than later. I'm building my portfolio."

Luis glanced at the card in Maryann's hand. "Fantastic! Well done, Tabitha. Please add me to your preferred vendors list. It's been wonderful working with you here, but I can't wait to see what you do on your own."

"You have more of those cards?"

Maryann asked. "I can hand them out to my bridal gown customers."

"Oh, my gosh! Yes, here take a whole stack." Tabitha gave Maryann at least fifty cards. Maybe four hundred wasn't such an ambitious order after all?

"Ooh, you know what?" Luis said. "My friends Juanita and Martin, their girl, Gladis, has her quinceañera coming up in June. They might be interested. Better give me some to hand out too."

Tabitha laughed. "You two are making this easy on me."

"We believe in you, kid," Maryann said, stowing the cards in the pocket of her camel-colored herringbone tweed pencil skirt. "You and Daphne."

"Hey peoples," Daphne said, sidling up to Tabitha. "I hope you don't mind my crashing this party with our newly engaged friends."

"What!?" Tabitha pulled Amos into a hug.

Petra held out her hand and they all ooh'd and ahh'd at her sparkly engagement ring.

Luis and Maryann held their hands out

again. "We did a thing too," Maryann said, winking at Petra.

"Finally!" Petra said, attack-hugging the happy couple.

"Is this a group hug or a game of Twister?" Daphne asked, caught in the middle.

The music merged from dancy-pop to a slow power ballad.

"I love this song," Luis, Petra, and Daphne said simultaneously.

The group moved out farther onto the dance floor, untangling themselves and pairing off.

Tabitha put her arms around her girlfriend's neck, while Daphne gripped Tabitha's hips.

Swaying to the music, they rested their foreheads against one another.

"Did you give out some cards?" Daphne asked.

"To Maryann and Luis," Tabitha said. "I'll have to get more out of my bag." She pulled her head back, her eyes locking on Daphne's. "But first..." Tabitha lowered her mouth to Daphne's, kissing her slowly, assuredly, with intermediate skills.

This time, no one interrupted.

I hope you enjoyed *Bright Smile*!

Check out the next book in the series -
Bright Day.

THREE YEARS AGO, billionaire Belle Walden
was sent on a secret mission to Braverton
by her vengeful grandfather. But instead of

acting on his wishes, Belle fell in love with Braverton, her job at the Secondhand Rose, and the person she's become while undercover.

WHEN BILLIONAIRE TYLER Day recognizes her at a party, she fears he'll call her out, but surprises her when he invites her to be his date at a charity gala.

AS THEY SPEND MORE and more time together, Belle questions if there's a better way to be a billionaire or if her feelings for Tyler are clouding her judgement.

EITHER WAY, her time in Braverton is ending, and she has to choose between family and fortune, or love and community, and Tyler isn't making her decision any easier.

ALSO BY ROXIE CLARKE

Old Town Braverton

<u>Pinwheel Plant Shop</u>

String of Hearts

Calico Hearts

Tangled Hearts

Christmas in Beaverton - Two Holiday Short Stories

Heart of Flame

Bleeding Heart

The Sweetheart Plant

Purple Heart

Old Town Braverton Box Set One

<u>Secondhand Rose Vintage Thrift Shop</u>

Bright Fire

Bright Smile

Bright Day

<u>Shopping for Love in Cataluma</u>

Inking the Deal

<u>**Tyler Creek Series**</u>

Forever My Favorite - FREE!

Forever and Always

Forever Merry Christmas

Forever My Home

<u>**Draper Falls Christmas Romance**</u>

Counting Down to Christmas

Catering to Christmas

Catching Up to Christmas

www.ingramcontent.com/pod-product-compliance
Lightning Source LLC
Chambersburg PA
CBHW031754150726
47989CB00006B/2715